For Stephanie • N.S.

For my parents • A.N.

First published by Candlewick Press

CANDLEWICK PRESS
2067 MASSACHUSETTS AVENUE
CAMBRIDGE MA 02140

ISBN 0-590-67982-1

Text copyright © 1954 by Norma Simon.
Illustrations copyright © 1995 by Alexi Natchev.
All rights reserved. Published by Scholastic Inc., 555 Broadway,
New York, NY 10012, by arrangement with Candlewick Press.

12 11 10 9 8 7 6 5 4 3 2 1   6 7 8 9/9 0 1/0

Printed in the U.S.A.   08

First Scholastic printing, March 1996

Norma Simon

WET WORLD

illustrated by Alexi Natchev

CANDLEWICK PRESS
CAMBRIDGE, MASSACHUSETTS

**A wet world waited
when I woke up
this morning**

wet windows

wet trees

wet leaves

wet rooftops

wet street

wet grass

wet world

A warm breakfast
waited when
I went down
the stairs

warm toast

warm cereal

warm cocoa

warm tummy

A stiff raincoat
slipped on my stiff arms

Shiny high boots
over my shiny shoes

Hat

coat

boots

Out to the
wet world

I walked on the wet world

Wet ground pulls my boots

Wet sidewalk splashes my boots

Wet rain sprinkles my hat

Wet rain drips down my coat

Wet cars swish down my road

Windshield wipers wipe the wet

Whish   whish
   whish   whish
      Whish away the wet

Wet puddles cover wet boots
Dry feet in wet boots
Dry arms in wet coat
Dry head in wet hat
Dry me
Wet world

A warm world waited when I went home
    warm mother
    warm father
    warm stove

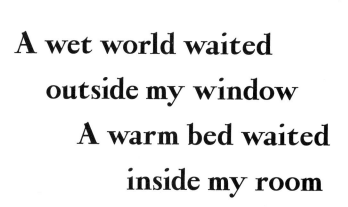

A wet world waited
outside my window
A warm bed waited
inside my room

A warm kiss kissed me
And now I'm in bed

I wonder what world

will wait in the morning

Good night
wet world

0-590-67982-1   SCHOLASTIC INC.   RL1 003